THE GREEN MACHINES

WAVE WARRIOR and the REEF RESCUE

For Frankie and the future of the oceans she loves so much– JS

For George – PC

For all life that exists on our blue planet and for
all of the people that depend on our seas – Greenpeace

First published in 2025 by Ivy Kids, an imprint of The Quarto Group.
1 Triptych Place, London, SE1 9SH, United Kingdom
T (0)20 7700 6700 F (0)20 7700 8066 **www.Quarto.com**
EEA Representation, WTS Tax d.o.o., Žanova ulica 3, 4000 Kranj, Slovenia.

A catalogue record for this book is available from the British Library.

ISBN: 978-1-8360-0392-2
eISBN: 978-1-8360-0394-6

The illustrations were created digitally
Set in Adobe Garamond and Just tell me what

Designer: Myrto Dimitrakoulia
Commissioning Editor: Georgia Buckthorn
Production controller: Dawn Cameron
Art Director: Karissa Santos
Publisher: Georgia Buckthorn and Peter Marley

Manufactured in the UK by Halstan & Co. Ltd. on recycled FSC® certified paper. HA012025
Printed by a company certified to ISO 14001: 2015
and carbon balanced in association with the World Land Trust.
1 3 5 7 9 8 6 4 2

FSC www.fsc.org RECYCLED Paper made from recycled material FSC® C019670

CARBON BALANCED PAPER www.carbonbalancedpaper.com

THE GREEN MACHINES

WAVE WARRIOR and the REEF RESCUE

JAMES SELLICK & PATRICK CORRIGAN

IN COLLABORATION WITH

GREENPEACE

IVY KIDS

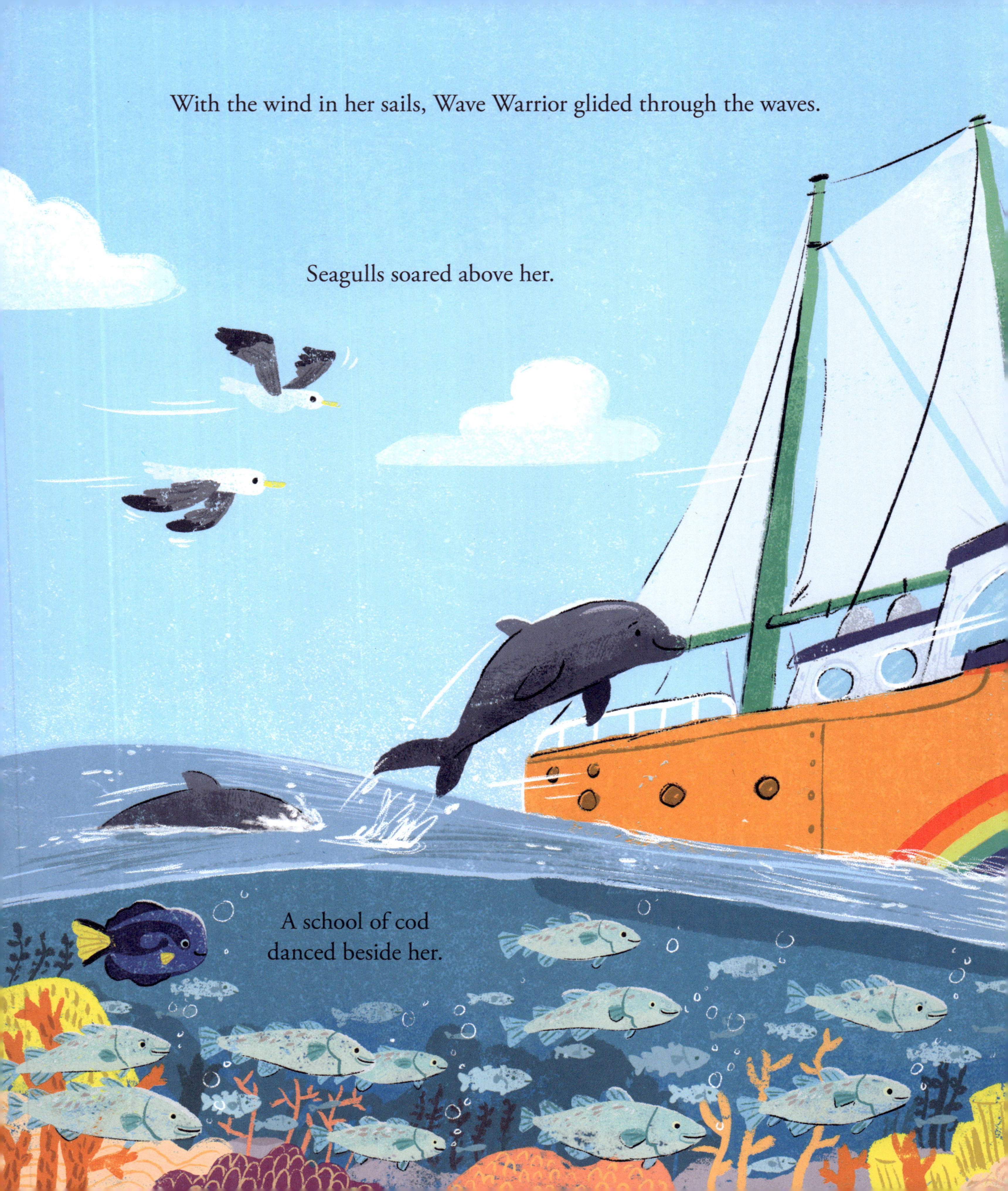

With the wind in her sails, Wave Warrior glided through the waves.

Seagulls soared above her.

A school of cod
danced beside her.

And a pod of porpoises
surfed in her wake.

All was calm off the Hope Island coast.

Wave Warrior then spotted the fishing trawler Codzilla up ahead.
"Codzilla must be lost," she presumed. "This is an ocean sanctuary!"

Out to the ***GIGANTINORMOUS*** trawler Wave Warrior sailed.

Excuse me, sir! You can't fish here. Your net is destroying Hope Reef!
Try and stop me!

Codzilla continued to drag his net along the seabed.

Codzilla's net caught creatures of all shapes and sizes.
Even creatures he didn't want!

Wave Warrior sailed into Codzilla's path.

But Codzilla was bigger than Wave Warrior.
He barged Wave Warrior to one side, leaving a crack in her hull.

"Well, if at first you don't succeed, try and try again," thought Wave Warrior.
She fired up her motor and chased Codzilla.

Codzilla was big, but his net slowed him down. Wave Warrior soon caught up.
She tried to get close enough to bite through Codzilla's net, but Codzilla had other ideas …

Codzilla snaked from side to side making it impossible.

"Codzilla is too big, too strong and too cunning!" thought Wave Warrior.
"I'll have to get help!"

Wave Warrior powered into Bliss Bay as fast as she could.
She frantically searched for someone who could help …

Wave Warrior waited and waited and waited.
Meanwhile, Codzilla continued to tear up more of Hope Reef.

Wave Warrior then spotted Hydronaut and Roboclaw.
They were building a flood defence wall out of boulders.

This gave Wave Warrior an idea …

"Please could I borrow some boulders?" asked Wave Warrior.
"Of course!" said Roboclaw.

Roboclaw lifted as many boulders as he could onto Wave Warrior.
She then powered back out to sea.

The boulders were so heavy, Wave Warrior worried she might sink.

One by one, Wave Warrior dropped the GIANT boulders overboard.

She didn't stop until all the boulders had been dropped.

Codzilla sniggered at Wave Warrior's feeble attempts to stop him.
Then, suddenly, he JOLTED to a halt …

Codzilla's net had caught on one of the boulders.

His net YANKED!

It STRETCHED!

Then, it TORE!

In a whirlwind of bubbles, the fish, sea creatures and birds escaped!

FREEDOM!

With his net in tatters, Codzilla retreated back out to sea.

But the crisis wasn't quite over. Codzilla had dumped his broken net overboard …

Willow was trapped!

HELP!

Willow's cries vibrated through the ocean.

COLOSSAL ... INCOMING!

Colossal the submarine had heard Willow's cries!
In one swift snip, Colossal cut through the net and freed Willow.

Wave Warrior then hauled in the net so it couldn't trap anyone else.

All was calm off the Hope Island coast once more.

Protected by the boulders, Hope Reef could begin to recover.

WHAT'S THE REAL STORY?

Industrial fishing is a big threat to the wildlife in our oceans. This is where large numbers of massive fishing trawlers like Codzilla have been catching too many fish and using gear that destroys ocean life. Together, they have already removed at least two-thirds of the large fish from our ocean. That's a lot of fish!

Many of them drag their nets along the seabed, which destroys everything in their way, including coral reefs. As well as fish, they catch thousands of 'unwanted' species called bycatch. This can include birds, turtles, whales, sharks, rays, porpoises and dolphins, many of which are endangered. To make things worse, these fishing trawlers sometimes dump their broken nets into the sea. These are called ghost nets and can dangerously trap sea creatures.

Fortunately, Wave Warrior was inspired by a real Greenpeace ship named Rainbow Warrior, who keeps a watchful eye on fishing trawlers to make sure they're not catching more than they're allowed. Rainbow Warrior also cleans up ghost nets, and Greempeace ships really do drop big boulders onto the seabed to protect it. But these are only partial solutions.

To really protect our oceans, Greenpeace and millions of others are fighting for more ocean sanctuaries. These are vast areas of protected water with strict limits on human activities like fishing. Lots of people have also committed to eating fewer fish, so their numbers can begin to replenish. It will take a long time for our oceans to fully recover, and there will be plenty of obstacles along the way, but like Wave Warrior, with every setback we'll grow stronger, more determined and more united than ever before.

Meet the Green Machines – the brave gang of vehicles working together to save Hope Island!

Also available:
Flamekraken and the Forest Fire

When a wildfire starts in Evergreen Forest, putting animals in danger, Flamekraken the fire engine is quick to respond. He battles the fire with every drop of water he has, but the fire continues to creep, crackle and roar. Just as Flamekraken starts to lose hope, his airborne buddy Heletor comes to the rescue.

A final note to parents from Greenpeace:

In these stories, machines are the heroes – but in real life, technology is only a small part of the solution. More than anything, we need to demand that governments and big businesses take action to protect our precious planet.

If you would like more guidance on how to talk to children about issues like climate change and support them to take action, please download our Greenpeace guide.